D0347163

My name is: .....Comet...................

My best friend is: .....My twin sister, Destiny..

My favourite colour is: ....Purple.............

My favourite food is: ......Hay..................

...I like to look after.....

...my sister

RAINBOW MIST SCHOOL
CLASS GOLDEN FEATHER

My name is: .....Destiny...................

My best friend is: .....My twin brother, Comet..

My favourite colour is: All the colours of the rainbow

My favourite food is: .....Grass.................

...I like to do dares and...

...get into mischief!

Sue Bentley's books for children often include animals, fairies and wildlife. She lives in Northampton and enjoys reading, going to the cinema and watching the birds on the feeders outside her window. She loves horses, which she thinks are all completely magical. One of her favourite books is *Black Beauty*, which she must have read at least ten times. At school she was always getting told off for daydreaming, but she now knows that she was storing up ideas for when she became a writer. Sue has met and owned many animals, but the wild creatures in her life hold a special place in her heart.

Sue Bentley

Pony Camp

PUFFIN

To Daisy-May – a challenge,

but always fun and warm-hearted

PUFFIN BOOKS

Published by the Penguin Group
Penguin Books Ltd, 80 Strand, London WC2R 0RL, England
Penguin Group (USA) Inc., 375 Hudson Street, New York, New York 10014, USA
Penguin Group (Canada), 90 Eglinton Avenue East, Suite 700, Toronto, Ontario, Canada M4P 2Y3
(a division of Pearson Penguin Canada Inc.)
Penguin Ireland, 25 St Stephen's Green, Dublin 2, Ireland (a division of Penguin Books Ltd)
Penguin Group (Australia), 250 Camberwell Road, Camberwell, Victoria 3124, Australia
(a division of Pearson Australia Group Pty Ltd)
Penguin Books India Pvt Ltd, 11 Community Centre, Panchsheel Park, New Delhi – 110 017, India
Penguin Group (NZ), 67 Apollo Drive, Rosedale, North Shore 0632, New Zealand
(a division of Pearson New Zealand Ltd)
Penguin Books (South Africa) (Pty) Ltd, 24 Sturdee Avenue, Rosebank,
Johannesburg 2196, South Africa

Penguin Books Ltd, Registered Offices: 80 Strand, London WC2R 0RL, England

puffinbooks.com

First published 2009
1

Text copyright © Sue Bentley, 2009
Illustrations copyright © Angela Swan, 2009
All rights reserved

The moral right of the author and illustrator has been asserted

Set in Bembo
Made and printed in England by Clays Ltd, St Ives plc

British Library Cataloguing in Publication Data
A CIP catalogue record for this book is available from the British Library

ISBN: 978-0-141-32773-0

www.greenpenguin.co.uk

Prologue

Comet folded his gold-feathered wings as he drifted down to land on Rainbow Mist Island. The grass was lush and velvety beneath his shining hooves. It felt good to be home.

But the magic pony's happiness faded as he thought of his twin sister. Destiny had been gone for so long. Surely she would have found her way back here by now.

He trotted hopefully up the slope towards a small wood. Comet's deep violet eyes scanned the trees for signs of movement. Maybe Destiny would be sheltering there from the hot sun.

Sunlight poured down on to his cream coat and flowing mane and tail, which glimmered like spun gold silk. Comet paused to drink from a spring that bubbled over shimmering, moss-covered rocks.

The nearby trees were covered in light-pink and violet leaves that rustled softly in the breeze. Suddenly the ground shook as thudding hooves approached. Was it another of Comet's Lightning Herd or one of the fierce dark horses? Comet tensed, ready to turn and flee, but then hesitated.

Perhaps it was his twin sister, hurrying to greet him!

'Destiny?'

An older horse with glowing dark eyes burst into the open. Its nostrils were flared and it was breathing hard.

'Blaze!' Comet greeted the leader of the Lightning Herd. 'What's wrong? Is Destiny with you?'

Blaze reared up on to his back legs. 'It was a dark horse, but the stone helped me outrun it!' As he grew calmer, his dark eyes softened. 'I am glad to see you again, my young friend. But I am afraid that Destiny has not come back.'

Disappointment flooded through Comet. 'She must think she is still in trouble.'

The Lightning Herd's Stone of Power

protected them from the dark horses who wanted to steal their magic. It had been lost while Comet and Destiny were playing a game of cloud-racing. Comet had found the stone again, but Destiny had already left.

'You must find her and tell her it is safe to return.' Blaze struck the grass with one shining front hoof and a fiery opal appeared.

As Comet drew closer, the Stone grew larger and multicoloured rays of light streamed out from it. In the centre an image formed. He saw a pony galloping across green fields in a world far away.

Comet's eyes widened. 'There she is!'

There was a flash of bright violet light and a drift of rainbow mist that swirled around the magic pony. Where the cream-coloured winged pony had stood there was now a glossy dark-brown Fell pony with a white star on his forehead.

'Go now. Use this disguise,' Blaze urged. 'Bring Destiny back safely!'

'I will,' Comet vowed.

He whinnied as he felt the power building within him. The swirling multicoloured mist thickened as it drew him in.

Chapter
ONE

Lindsey Heaven's heart thudded
uncomfortably as the car and horsebox
turned in through the imposing stone
gates. Acres of open fields and woodland
stretched away on either side. Hamilton
Hall, a large stone building, was on a hill
in the distance.

A sign pointing the other way read
'Hamilton Riding'.

'Look at that view!' Mr Heaven exclaimed as he headed towards the riding centre. 'I bet you're already imagining going for a ride on Allsorts.'

'Mmm,' Lindsey murmured vaguely, feeling another flutter of nerves.

Allsorts was Lindsey's pony. It had been her mum and dad's idea for her to come to pony camp. They thought she spent too much time alone and needed to meet more kids of her own age. And they weren't sure if they could afford to keep Allsorts for much longer and wanted Lindsey to enjoy camp with her own pony.

'Ah, here we are.' Mr Heaven spotted a number of small log cabins through the trees.

'Lindsey is in number four,' Mrs Heaven said. 'There it is, over there. It'll be fun to sleep in a cabin. They look really cosy.'

My bedroom's even cosier, Lindsey thought, wishing she was there right now.

She took a deep breath as she nervously imagined having to share with other kids. She hoped they'd be easy to get on with. She really did want to try to make new friends.

They pulled up in front of the rows of

cabins and her dad got her case out of the boot. There were cars and horseboxes everywhere. Lindsey could see kids through open cabin doors, dumping their cases, calling out greetings and choosing beds.

A slim woman with a blonde ponytail seemed to be in charge. She smiled at Lindsey. 'Hi! I'm Gina Morgan, chief instructor. Welcome to Hamilton Riding.'

Lindsey smiled shyly. 'Thank you,' she said politely. 'I'm Lindsey Heaven.'

The woman ticked her name off on a clipboard. 'Go right in, Lindsey. Two of your cabin-mates have arrived and the other's been held up, but is on her way. You can start getting to know each other while your parents take your pony to the stable.'

Lindsey swallowed hard. 'You'll . . . you'll come and say goodbye before you leave, won't you?'

'Of course we will!' Mrs Heaven patted her daughter's arm. 'Off you go now. We'll see to Allsorts.'

'Thanks, Mum. Tell him I'll come and give him a cuddle later.'

Lindsey watched the car and horsebox pulling away and then went into the cabin. Sunlight was pouring in through two large windows. Four beds were in the roomy cabin, one placed either side of each window. Bright yellow curtains and checked bedclothes made the room cheerful and welcoming.

Two girls had already claimed the beds nearest to the bathroom door. They were unpacking cases and folding clothes into chests of drawers.

One of them turned round. She was
tall and pretty with shiny brown hair and
fashionable-looking clothes. She seemed
about eleven years old. 'I'm Natasha
Smart, but I only speak to people if they
call me Tash,' she said curtly.

'Erm . . . Hi, Tash. I'm Lindsey, but
everyone calls me Lins,' Lindsey replied,
a bit thrown by Natasha's abruptness.

Tash just nodded towards the other girl.
'That's Shawna, and just so you know,
she's *my* best friend.'

Lindsey's heart sank. It was obvious Tash didn't care about making friends like she did. This was turning out to be just like school. She wandered sadly over to one of the spare beds.

'This place is cool, isn't it?' Shawna said. Freckles dotted her pale skin and she wore her long red hair in a plait.

'Um . . . yeah, it seems really nice –' Lindsey began, in an effort to be friendly to the other older girl. But then she realized that Shawna was talking to Tash.

'Duh!' Tash mocked. 'What a muppet!' The girls giggled and rolled their eyes.

Lindsey felt herself blushing and wished the floor would open up and swallow her. Unpopping her case, she tried to ignore the other girls as she began loading her clothes into her bedside chest.

'So, which pony camps have you been to?' Shawna called out. 'Hey! You listening?'

Lindsey realized that she was being spoken to this time. 'I haven't been to camp before. This is my first one.'

'Oh great!' Tash snorted. 'We're stuck with a camp newbie! Are you any good at riding?'

Lindsey's cheeks were practically burning. She knew she must be as red as a beetroot. 'I'm . . . um, OK, I think,' she said modestly. The riding-school owner said she was actually pretty good, but Lindsey didn't like to boast.

'Well, you'd better be! We don't want any lame ducks, losing us team points!' Tash retorted.

Shawna laughed and chucked her

pillow at Tash. 'I'm done unpacking. Let's go explore!'

Linking arms, the friends wandered out together.

'See you later,' Lindsey called, but neither of them answered. The cabin door slammed shut in her face.

She plonked herself down on to her bed. How was she going to get through the next week, with those two? Shawna was tolerable, but Tash was an absolute horror. She just hoped that the final girl, who had yet to arrive, would be nicer than they were.

Lindsey was still sitting there, when her mum and dad came to say goodbye. 'Everything's sorted. Allsorts is in his stall and you can go and see him whenever you like,' her mum told her.

Her dad ruffled her short brown hair.
'So we'll be off now. See you next week.
Have a wonderful time. And we'll phone
you in the morning.'

There was a horrible sinking feeling
in Lindsey's tummy and she only just
managed to stop herself begging to be

taken home with them. Instead she gave them a big hug and said her goodbyes. Outside the cabin, she waved until their car was out of sight.

Sighing heavily, she wondered what to do next. Finally, she decided to go and find the stables. There was a path through the woods and some buildings in the distance. She set off through the trees.

Lindsey was only just out of sight of the cabin when she reached a clearing. There was a sudden bright flash and a patch of glittering multicoloured mist appeared, which filled the whole area in front of her. She noticed rainbow droplets twinkling on her bare arms.

'Oh!' Lindsey screwed up her face, trying to see through the strange mist.

As it slowly cleared, she spotted a pretty

dark-brown Fell pony, with a white star on its forehead, walking towards her.

'Can you help me, please?' it asked in a velvety whinny.

Chapter
TWO

Lindsey's eyes widened as she stared at the pretty pony in complete astonishment.

She didn't know what a loose pony was doing in the woods, but she did know that it couldn't possibly talk to her! She shook her head slowly, thinking that she must be imagining things.

She walked towards it, with her hands at her sides so she wouldn't alarm it.

'Hello, there,' she said, in a soft encouraging voice. 'Aren't you gorgeous? How did you manage to escape? I bet everyone's looking for you. I'd better find the stables and take you back there.'

The pony's ears twitched and it lifted its head proudly. 'I did not escape from anywhere. I have just arrived here from Rainbow Mist Island.'

Lindsey stopped in her tracks. 'Y-you really c-can talk?' she stuttered. 'Or is this some kind of trick?'

She looked round nervously, expecting to see Tash hiding behind a tree, ready to jump out and make fun of her. It seemed like the kind of thing she might do. But there was no one in sight.

She turned back to the pony, frowning in puzzlement. For the first time, she

noticed that it had unusual deep violet
eyes.

'I am Comet of the Lightning Horses.
May I know your name?' it neighed
politely.

Lindsey blinked, finally having to
accept that something totally amazing was
happening. 'I'm . . . I'm Lindsey Heaven,
but everyone calls me Lins. I'm here at
pony camp.'

Comet dipped his head in a formal
bow and his dark brown mane fell

forward. 'I am honoured to meet you, Lins.'

Lindsey hesitated. Should she curtsy or something? She settled for awkwardly leaning forward. 'Um . . . me too.' Her curiosity was starting to take over from her shock. 'No offence, but why did you come here?'

Comet snorted and twitched his tail. 'I am looking for my twin sister who is lost and in hiding. She is called Destiny.'

Lindsey looked round for another magic pony, but this part of the woods was empty except for her and Comet. 'But why is Destiny in hiding? Is someone after her?' she asked.

Comet's neck drooped a little with sadness. 'We were playing cloud-racing in the night sky, when Destiny accidentally lost the Stone of Power. The stone protects the Lightning Herd from the dark horses who want to steal our magic. I found it again, but Destiny had already left. Now she is far away from the stone's protection and in danger of being found by the dark horses.'

Lindsey listened hard. It all sounded so magical and strange. But one thing he said was bothering her. 'You and Destiny were cloud-racing? In the sky? But how –'

'Please stay there,' Comet whinnied, backing away.

Lindsey felt a warm prickling sensation like pins and needles flowing through her fingers right to the tips. Violet sparkles bloomed in Comet's dark-brown coat and a light rainbow mist whirled around him. The pretty Fell pony disappeared and in his place stood a large, regal cream-coloured pony, with a flowing golden mane and tail. Springing from his shoulders were magnificent, gleaming gold-feathered wings.

Lindsey gasped. Nothing could have

prepared her for such a beautiful sight. She was speechless with wonder.

'Comet?' she gulped, when she could finally speak.

'Yes, it is still me, Lins. There is nothing to fear,' Comet said in a deep musical neigh. There was a final flash and a swirl of glittering mist and Comet reappeared as a pretty dark-brown pony with a white star on his forehead.

'Wow! That's a brilliant disguise. Can Destiny do that too?'

Comet nodded. 'But no disguise will save her if our enemies discover her,' he snorted gravely. 'I must look for her. Will you help me?'

Lindsey felt a flicker of doubt. The dark horses sounded fierce and dangerous. What would a nervous scaredy-cat like

her be able to do against them? But then
the magic pony came right up to her.
Leaning forward, he pushed his satiny
nose into her hand.

Lindsey's heart melted as she felt
Comet huffing warm breath on to her
fingers. 'Of course I will – we'll search for
Destiny together.'

'Thank you, Lins.'

'Just wait until you meet Tash and Shawna. That'll show them who's . . .'

Comet laid back his ears. 'No! I am sorry, Lins. You can tell no one about me or what I have told you!'

Lindsey was confused. It was going to be pretty hard to keep Comet a secret. A loose pony that didn't belong to anyone was bound to attract attention. She told Comet this.

'You must promise,' the magic pony insisted. 'All will be well, Lins.'

As Lindsey looked into his intelligent eyes, she felt a warm, happy glow spread through her and realized that she trusted him completely. 'Well – OK then,' she agreed, smiling. 'Cross my heart.'

'Thank you, Lins.'

'I'll try to slip away and meet you later, once I find out how things work here,' she told him. 'This place is huge. There are acres of fields and woods with lakes where Destiny could be hiding.'

Suddenly a loud voice rang out.

'What*ever* are you doing, talking to yourself? You're a bit old to have an imaginary friend, aren't you?'

Lindsey looked up to see Tash coming towards her. She took a deep breath. How was she going to explain about Comet?

'Um . . . I was just –' she began.

'Duh! Save it for someone who's interested,' Tash interrupted rudely. 'I'm missing out on the yummy welcome tea, because I was sent to find you! We're in the Hay Net restaurant. So, hurry up, right?' She whirled round and jogged

away in the direction of a large building,
just visible through the trees.

'Yeah, OK. I'll be . . . er, right there!'
Lindsey called after her.

She was confused. Why hadn't Tash said
something about the dark-brown Fell
pony, who stood there as large as life?
It was almost as if she hadn't noticed him.
Lindsey didn't get it.

When she turned back to Comet,
she saw that his large violet eyes were
glowing with amusement. 'I used my

magic so that only you will be able to see and hear me,' he explained.

'You can make yourself invisible? Oh well! That makes things loads easier!' she exclaimed. Reaching out she scratched gently at the white star between Comet's eyes. She smiled as he lowered his head in enjoyment.

Her lonely stay at pony camp with two awful cabin-mates looked like being a lot more fun now that she had the magic pony for a special friend!

Chapter
THREE

Tash had been right about one thing. The tea in the Hay Net was delicious. Lindsey polished off masses of sandwiches, scones and a huge slice of yummy chocolate gateau.

Everyone around her was chatting and laughing. Lots of them seemed to know each other from previous pony camps. No one paid her much attention, but Lindsey didn't mind so much now. She was used to it and, anyway, she couldn't wait to go back to the woods to see Comet, even if it was just to prove to herself that she hadn't dreamt the whole thing.

She stood up and began weaving her way through the tables.

'Off to have another chat with your imaginary friend?' Tash called after her.

Lindsey half-turned, blushing again. She hated being teased, especially as she could never think of a clever reply.

'I'm going to . . . finish unpacking,' she murmured, looking down at the floor. *Actually I'm going to meet my magic pony friend. But you wouldn't believe me, even if I told you. Which I'm never going to!*

'Unpacking. Wow! That's so exciting!' Tash smirked, giving Shawna a dig.

Unfortunately for Shawna, she had a big mouthful of the chocolate gateau and Lindsey almost laughed out loud as she spluttered half the cake back on to the table.

Lindsey soon forgot about Tash and Shawna as she eagerly hurried through the woods until she reached the place where Comet had appeared.

'Comet!' she whispered.

There was no answer.

She walked through the trees, looking

to the right and the left and then retraced
her steps to look again. But the dark-
brown Fell pony wasn't there. Lindsey's
spirits fell. Maybe Comet had changed
his mind about being her friend and had
found someone else to help him search
for Destiny.

She decided to come back later just in
case Comet had returned. She desperately
hoped so. Her shoulders slumped a little
in disappointment at not seeing her
special friend, as she walked back to the
cabin.

Lindsey emerged from the trees to see a
girl standing outside her cabin. As the girl
bent to pick up her suitcase, the handle
came off in her hand.

Thump! There was a loud clatter as the
suitcase fell to the ground. It burst open

and the contents spilled out.

'Oh heck!' the girl groaned loudly. 'First our car breaks down and we have to wait about a hundred years for the breakdown truck. And now my useless suitcase dies on me!'

Lindsey hurried towards her. 'Let me help you,' she offered, already scrambling about on the floor to gather up scattered socks, T-shirts and knickers.

'Oh, thanks. I didn't know anyone was there.' Smiling, the girl tucked a strand of light-brown hair behind one ear. She had a round face and lively brown eyes. 'I'm Penny. Penny Cookson.'

'Hi, Penny. I'm Lindsey. You must be our fourth cabin-mate'

'I am!' Penny declared. 'And I'm so hungry I could eat a grizzly bear squashed between two mattresses. I bet I've rotten well missed tea too, haven't I?'

Lindsey nodded, grinning, as she opened the door and dumped an armful of stuff on to the empty bed. 'Yeah, 'fraid so. It was pretty good too, especially the cake. We could go and see if there's anything left. I can show you where the Hay Net is. That's the restaurant, where we have all our meals.'

36

'That would be great! I just have to put these out first.' Opening a zip-up bag, Penny took out a collection of model ponies and lined them up on top of her bedside chest.

'Wow! Those are really cute!' Lindsey admired the tiny pretty faces, bright glass eyes and silky manes and tails. 'They're so lifelike. Have they got names?'

'You bet! This one's Spot and that's Fudge and this one's my favourite, Petal the Palomino ...' Penny had just finished reeling off the names of all the tiny horses when Tash and Shawna came in.

Tash took one look at the messy heap of clothes and other stuff. 'You'd better clear that up, right now!' she said, bossily. 'We lose team points for leaving the cabin in a mess.'

Lindsey felt bad for the new girl. She'd hardly set foot in the place and Tash was having a go at her. 'It wasn't Penny's fault!' She forgot to be shy as she defended the new girl. 'Her suitcase bur—'

Tash glared at her. 'What's it got to do with you?'

Penny gently put a hand on Lindsey's arm. 'Thanks, but it's OK,' she said softly, before turning to Tash. 'So where's your badge?'

'Huh? What badge?' Tash looked puzzled.

'The one that says, "I'm in charge"!' Penny quipped.

Tash looked taken aback for a moment. 'I was only saying!' she countered and then her eyes gleamed spitefully. 'What sort of a name's Penny, anyway? Who'd

want to be called after a measly cheap
brown coin?'

'That's a good one, Tash!' Shawna
tittered.

'Tash?' Penny said, her mouth
twitching. 'You can talk! You're named
after a bit of fuzz under a man's nose!'

'I am not!' Tash spluttered, going red.
'Tash is short for Natasha!'

'Ooh, I *do* beg your pudden!' Penny
mocked, in a stuffy old-fashioned voice.
'Well, I'd love to chat, but I've got some
clearing up to do.' Ignoring Tash and

Shawna, she began opening drawers and
stuffing handfuls of clothes inside.

Tash stood there open-mouthed.
Moments later, she flounced over to her
bed with Shawna in tow.

Lindsey bit back a grin as she looked
at Penny in admiration. She didn't want
to hope too much that she'd met a real
friend but, either way, she was a whole lot
nicer than either Tash or Shawna!

As her cabin-mates got ready for bed,
Lindsey fidgeted impatiently. After visiting
Allsorts in the stable that evening to make
sure the black-and-white pony was settled
in, she'd cut back through the woods,
looking for Comet. But there was still
no sign of the magic pony. She lay there
trying to think of an excuse to go back

outside again, but nothing came to mind.

Tash and Shawna were lying on their beds in their pyjamas, chatting and flipping through pony magazines, and Penny was in the bathroom. Lindsey sighed. It looked as if she was going to have to wait until the other girls were asleep before she could slip out.

Only half-concentrating, she reached for the book on the top of her bedside chest. Her fingers brushed lightly against a tiny model pony.

Lindsey frowned. Weird. What was one of Penny's models doing near her bed?

She looked more closely at the tiny pony, which was dark brown with a white star on its forehead and big deep violet eyes. It looked a lot like . . .

The model pony suddenly shook itself

and its ears twitched forward.

'Comet?' Lindsey gasped. 'Is it really you? What are you doing here?'

'I was waiting for you to come and meet me in the woods and I saw how many people there are at pony camp,' he told her in tiny soft neigh that matched his new size. 'I thought it might be difficult for you to sneak out without being seen. So this seemed like a better way for us to be together.'

'And it's much more fun!' Lindsey whispered delightedly. She felt a surge of affection for her magical friend. He was so thoughtful. 'This is so cool! Now you can sleep on my bed and be warm and cosy if it rains. And I can take you everywhere with me in my bag. You can even ride Allsorts with me.'

Comet whinnied with pleasure. 'I would like that. And we can look for Destiny at the same time.'

'You've thought of everything!' Lindsey said. Comet was full of surprises. She wondered what else her magic friend could do.

Reaching out, she gently picked him up and then sat with him in her lap. Comet was pretty as a dark-brown Fell pony and magnificent as his beautiful golden-winged self – but right now he was the cutest, most adorable toy pony imaginable.

She was so busy stroking his tiny ears and petal-soft coat and admiring his tiny perfect hooves that she didn't notice Tash watching her with raised eyebrows.

Suddenly Tash bounded across the room. 'What are you doing with Penny's toy pony? I bet you didn't ask her if you could have it.'

Before Lindsey could stop her she grabbed Comet roughly. The tiny pony gave a whinny of dismay as Tash walked off with him.

Chapter
FOUR

Lindsey froze, waiting for Tash to notice that Comet was real. But, just like in the woods, when Tash hadn't been able to see Comet at all, she now seemed only to be able to see him as a normal toy.

Lindsey realized that his secret was still safe. But she didn't know whether his magic would protect him from being hurt. Tash was holding him so tightly he could hardly breathe. She had to get him back.

Leaping off the bed, Lindsey launched herself across the room. 'Comet's not Penny's. He's mine! Give him back!' she demanded.

'Make me!' Tash crowed, holding him in the air.

Lindsey tried to jump up and grab Comet, but Tash was taller than she was and she couldn't reach.

Tash tossed the toy towards Shawna. 'Here! Catch!'

Lindsey heard Comet give a tiny frightened neigh as Shawna just managed to grab him by one leg.

'Stop it! You'll hurt him!' As she ran towards her, Shawna laughed and tossed Comet back to Tash.

'Oops!' Tash fumbled her catch and
Comet was launched right up into the air.

Lindsey backed up, positioning
herself to catch him as he plummeted
downwards. *Yes! Got him!* Comet was safe,
but as she turned, clutching him tightly,
she banged heavily into a chair and
twisted her ankle.

'Ow!' Tears of pain stung her eyes, but
she swallowed hard, determined not to
cry in front of the older girls. Holding
Comet close, she hobbled over to her
bed and sat down. 'Are you OK?' she
whispered, stroking him very gently.

Comet's tiny eyes glittered like
amethysts. 'I am not hurt, thanks to you.
You were brave to save me from those
two mean girls.'

'I wasn't really. I just couldn't bear

anything to happen to you,' Lindsey said.
Now that the excitement was over, her
ankle began throbbing painfully and she
bit her lip.

'You have hurt yourself. Let me help,'
Comet neighed.

Lindsey felt a tingling sensation
flowing to the very tips of her fingers as

miniature violet sparks glowed in the tiny pony's coat and a glittering rainbow mist full of tiny multicoloured stars swirled around her ankle. Gradually the coloured mist sank into her pyjama leg and then disappeared, as did every last one of the tiny violet sparks.

'Oh! My ankle feels fine now. Thanks, Comet,' Lindsey said. She swung her legs up and lay back against her pillows, still holding him close.

'Honestly! Some people can't take a joke,' Tash scoffed. Lindsey refused to even meet her gaze. 'Collecting stupid model ponies is pathetic anyway.'

The bathroom door opened. Penny came out and stood in the cabin with her hands on her hips. 'Did I hear someone say that collecting model ponies is pathetic?' she asked, looking pointedly towards Tash.

Tash's expression changed. 'Er . . . no! It's great. I love model ponies,' Tash fibbed, hurriedly jumping into bed.

Penny came and got into bed too. 'Night, Lindsey,' she said, switching off her bedside lamp.

'Night, Penny. Night, Comet,' Lindsey whispered happily, cradling him close as she snuggled up with him under the duvet.

Over breakfast in the Hay Net the following morning, Penny was trying to cheer Lindsey up after her mum and dad had called with bad news about Allsorts. They were going to have to sell him as soon as possible. Lindsey was feeling

incredibly sad. It seemed like things were
going from bad to worse! She wondered
if Comet would come home to live with
her – perhaps she would ask him later on.

'It *would* be best-turned-out pony first,'
Penny joked, trying to cheer Lindsey up.
'I'm rubbish at cleaning tack. It always
looks worse than it did before I started.'

Lindsey smiled gratefully, as she chewed
on a bit of toast. She had one hand on
Comet, who sat on her lap, out of sight
beneath the table. 'Don't worry, I'll help

you. I'm a total whizz with a damp
sponge and a tin of saddle soap!'

Penny laughed. 'You're on!'

A cheerful buzz of voices and laughter
filled the big, light room. The delicious
smell of bacon cooking wafted from the
self-service counter. Tash and Shawna
were sitting on a nearby table. Looking
over at Lindsey and Penny, they nudged
each other and whispered. Lindsey just
knew they were talking about Allsorts.

'Those two are awful!' Penny said,
shaking her head.

'I know. I try to ignore them,' Lindsey
said, reaching down to stroke Comet's
tiny silky mane.

'I am going to become normal size
now, Lins. I will see you outside later,'
Comet whickered softly and disappeared

in a little burst of invisible violet sparkles.

Lindsey and Penny finished eating and began strolling towards the tack room together. 'Shall we go and say hello to our ponies first?' Lindsey suggested.

'You bet. I can't wait to ride Chance,' Penny told her. 'Wait until you see her. She's so pretty and she does anything I ask her.'

Penny's blue-roan mare was in the stall opposite to where Allsorts stood with his head hanging over his door. Lindsey gave him a cuddle. 'Hello, boy. How do you like your stable?'

Penny was giving Chance a peppermint. The pony had large kind eyes and a neat head with a slightly dished nose.

'What a lovely pony. Have you had her

for long?' Lindsey asked.

'About a year or so. I'm looking for a sharer for her,' Penny said. She kissed her pony's soft muzzle. 'How about you?' she asked.

But before Lindsey could answer, Tash's mocking tones filled the stable. 'Ugh. Check Penny, kissing her horse – imagine all the germs she has! Gross.'

'Well, I'd rather kiss Chance than kiss

you any day, *Natasha*,' Penny replied stressing Tash's full name that she hated so much.

Tash paused in the doorway and turned. She narrowed her eyes and gave Penny a really dirty look, before pressing her lips together and stomping away.

Lindsey felt a prickle of unease. 'You shouldn't wind her up, Penny,' she warned.

'What's she going to do – nag me to death?' Penny said, laughing.

Lindsey grinned and forgot all about Tash as she and Penny strolled towards the tack room. 'So, about cleaning tack,' she started explaining. 'First we have to take it all apart . . .'

Chapter
FIVE

At first, Lindsey found it strange to have Comet beside her when no one else could see the magic pony. Once or twice, during the activities, she almost turned to talk to him, but managed to catch herself just in time.

It was late in the afternoon before everyone was given a couple of hours of free time to do what they liked. Lindsey

seized on it eagerly. It was her first chance
to help Comet search for Destiny.

But Penny had other ideas. 'I'll just get
a drink then we can go out for a hack.
OK?' she enthused.

'Um . . . OK,' Lindsey murmured, taken
by surprise. She stared after Penny as
the other girl disappeared into the stable
kitchen.

She felt torn. If she went hacking with
Penny and Chance, she wouldn't be able to
help Comet. But she'd already promised
they could go and look for Destiny.

She had seconds to decide what to do
before Penny emerged.

'Follow me, Comet.' On impulse,
Lindsey mounted Allsorts and quickly
rode off, with Comet following closely
behind.

But as she glanced over her shoulder, she saw Penny standing in the doorway. 'Hey! Lins! Wait up!' she cried, looking hurt and puzzled.

'I'm sorry! I won't be long.' Lindsey felt bad. But she had no choice except to keep on going, if she wanted to avoid awkward questions. She would just have to try to make things up with Penny later and hope Penny understood.

Lindsey pointed Allsorts towards the bridle path that led through the woods. Comet pounded along beside them, his shining hooves making no sound. He whinnied at Allsorts and the little pony nickered back. Lindsey smiled as the two ponies made friends.

'I hope you haven't been too bored, hanging about all day,' she said to Comet.

'It has been very interesting,' he neighed.
'I liked it when Penny waved her arms
about and did a little dance.'

'That was when she got top marks
for best-turned-out pony,' she answered
Comet. 'The instructor said Penny's tack
was practically glowing and she needed
sunglasses to look at it!'

Comet swished his tail. 'It was kind
of you to help her with her tack. I like
Penny. She seems like a nice girl.'

'Yeah, she is. I wish I was as funny and confident as she is. Nothing fazes her.' *Not like me*, she thought, feeling another pang of guilt at having ridden off and left Penny standing. 'Anyway, let's go looking for Destiny!' Lindsey said, changing the subject. She felt better at the thought of spending some time helping Comet at last.

Comet tossed his head and pawed at the ground with one front hoof. As he leapt forward, Lindsey kicked Allsorts on. The little black-and-white pony snorted and quickened his pace.

The ponies galloped along side by side, Comet matching his longer stride to Allsorts', and Lindsey felt happiness glow through her as they sped along. Sunshine filtered down through the trees, casting spots of golden light on to them.

They wove along the bridle paths,
now and then passing other ponies and
riders who waved and smiled. Slowing
to a walk, Comet's keen eyes continually
searched for signs of his lost twin.

At one point during their ride, they
spotted a donkey and three ponies in a
small paddock beside a cottage. Comet
trotted up to them excitedly, his ears
pricking. But none of them was Destiny.

As Lindsey reached Comet she saw
that his violet eyes had lost a little of their
glow and his head was drooping slightly
with disappointment. He must be missing
Destiny badly. Her heart moved with
sympathy for her friend.

'We'll find her, don't worry,' she
reassured him. 'This camp is huge.

There're tons of places where Destiny
could be hiding. She might even have
come past here recently.'

'I would have known if she had,'
Comet neighed. 'She would have left a
trail.'

'A trail? What would it look like?'

'It would be a line of softly glowing
hoof-prints. But most humans would not
be able to see it.'

Lindsey was fascinated. 'Will I be able

to see it?'

Comet nodded. 'Yes. If you are riding me or we are very close.'

'Cool! That should make it easier to find her. Maybe, when you do, you could both come and live with me,' she said hopefully. 'I'll be going home from camp in a few days. You'll like it where I live.'

'I am afraid that is not possible,' Comet neighed. 'I must take Destiny back to our family on Rainbow Mist Island. I hope you understand, Lins.'

Lindsey nodded mutely as she forced herself to accept that Comet would not be staying forever. But she didn't want to think about that. He was here now and she wanted to enjoy every single moment with him.

'Shall we go on searching?' she said.

'What about over there? That looks like a farm up on that hill.'

Comet nodded and glanced around with renewed interest as they set off again. After a long, steep ride, they crested the hill. But they had no luck with the farm and its outbuildings and paused to look down into the valley before they went on.

Allsorts was panting and his sides were heaving. Lindsey decided she'd better take the little black–and–white pony back.

'He's willing to go on, but I've ridden him quite hard. I think he needs a drink and then to rest and cool down,' she reasoned.

Comet neighed agreement. 'Allsorts is a fine pony. He has done well. But if you were to ride me, we would be able to cover more ground and search for longer.'

Lindsey realized that he was right,
but it was always going to be difficult to
slip away by herself without someone
noticing and asking awkward question.
'I think there's a film show one night.
Everyone will be there. That would be
a good time to sneak out to meet you.'

'Thank you, Lins.'

Lindsey smiled at him, feeling like the
luckiest girl in the world. She was really
looking forward to riding her very own
magic pony friend.

Chapter
SIX

Lindsey left Comet nibbling the sweet grass on the hillside. As soon as she had given Allsorts a drink and rubbed him down, she went looking for Penny.
She found her sitting in the day room, flipping through a magazine and looking a bit bored.

Lindsey went over to her. 'Hi, what are you doing?' she asked quietly. She really hoped Penny wasn't too mad at her for riding off earlier.

Penny looked up. 'Oh, hi. I came here for a bit of peace. Tash, Shawna and a couple of other girls are having a picnic outside the cabin.'

'Didn't you fancy the picnic?'

Penny rolled her eyes. 'With Tash bossing everyone about? I'd rather sit in a bath of cold rice pudding!'

Lindsey burst out laughing. Penny said such funny things.

A serious expression crossed the other girl's face. 'Didn't you hear me calling you earlier on? I thought we were going hacking together?'

'Oh, I . . . er, wasn't sure if you meant it!' She spread her hands apologetically. 'I'm so sorry. I messed up.'

Penny's face cleared and she smiled. 'Don't worry about it. I ended up exploring round by the big lake. It was great to give Chance a good long ride. Maybe we can go hacking in the woods together another time?'

'Definitely,' Lindsey said, relieved. Thank goodness Penny had accepted her explanation. She would have hated to upset her, especially now it seemed they really were becoming friends, but at the same time she had to keep her promise to Comet.

It rained heavily overnight and it was still raining the following morning. There were puddles everywhere and the ground squelched beneath Lindsey's riding boots as she made her way to the stable yard.

Inside, Lindsey reached for the body brush from Allsorts' grooming kit by his stall and began working on his black– and-white coat with long, firm strokes.

The stable gradually filled up with other kids. Sounds of laughter, pony noises and rustling hay filled the air. Penny came in not long afterwards to groom Chance and the two girls chatted

as they worked. Soon their ponies' coats
were gleaming.

Lindsey admired Chance's unusual
blue-roan coat. 'She's so gorgeous. Your
sharer is going be a lucky rider.'

Penny nodded. 'It might be a bit
difficult to find one. We're moving house
to Blakestone soon after I get back from
camp.'

'Blakestone! But that's only a few miles away from where I live!' Lindsey said delightedly.

Before Penny could reply, Gina Morgan walked in. 'Listen up, everyone. We'll be doing stable management today and schooling work in the yard tomorrow,' she announced. 'Cross-country and team games will take place when the weather's better. Sorry, but we'll be mostly indoors today, guys.'

There were a few groans of disappointment at not being able to go out riding on the ponies.

Lindsey had been looking forward to riding Allsorts, with Comet galloping alongside them again as they both kept an eye out for Destiny. She hoped Comet had found somewhere dry to shelter until this awful weather broke.

'Greetings, Lins,' his soft neigh sounded close to her and she felt his breath ruffle her hair.

'Oh!' She almost jumped out of her skin.

Lindsey bit back a grin as she turned and saw Comet's head hanging over the door of an empty stall behind her. His deep violet eyes were glinting cheekily. She wished she could give her invisible magic pony a hug, but she daren't risk it with so many people in the stable.

Gina was now talking about skips, brushes and hay forks. 'It's good practice to get used to putting things away. Leaving things lying around can cause accidents to you *and* your pony . . .'

'No one can tell *me* anything about

stable management,' Tash boasted. She looked sideways at Lindsey. 'You learn loads from looking after your *own* pony. I've been taking care of Jewel ever since Dad bought him.' Jewel was her showy black thoroughbred gelding.

Lindsey tried to ignore Tash's comment, but she knew the other girl was referring to her losing Allsorts soon. She chewed at her bottom lip.

'Is something wrong, Lins?' Comet whinnied.

'It's Tash. She's such a pain. I've had enough of her sly digs at me!' she whispered angrily.

Comet twitched his ears thoughtfully.

'Muck heaps,' Gina said. 'Not very glamorous maybe, but they're a fact of life for pony lovers. They can easily spread out of control, unless you're firm with them. Right?'

There was a ripple of agreement.

'The thing to do is to give some thought about building them up. It's not enough to tip your wheelbarrow and run away. You want a muck heap with a dip in the centre, like a saucer, not heaped up like a soggy pudding. So it's build and squash – jump up and down on it every day.'

'Anyone knows *that*!' Tash commented to Shawna.

The instructor looked at her. 'If you're such an expert, why don't you demonstrate for the rest of us? There's a wheelbarrow of soiled bedding over there.'

'Sure!' Tash smiled confidently. She took hold of the handles and wheeled the light plastic barrow to the muck heap across the yard. Everyone watched as she pushed it up the steep ramp.

Lindsey felt a familiar tingling feeling flow down her fingers as violet sparkles glinted in Comet's dark-brown coat, and a fine rainbow mist, invisible to everyone but Lindsey, swirled around Tash and the wheelbarrow. *What's he up to?* she wondered.

The rainbow mist dissolved into glittery dust and disappeared. Suddenly the barrow seemed to give a jaunty little skip and tipped backwards. The pile of smelly hay teetered. And a huge wodge of hay and pongy poo fell, splattering all over Tash.

Everyone fell about laughing.

'Oh, Comet. That was naughty!' Lindsey spluttered. 'But she deserved it!'

Penny was helpless with laughter.

'Oh dear,' the instructor said, her lips twitching. 'Are you all right, Tash?'

'No! This is my best designer polo top!' Tash said through gritted teeth. She stalked back out to the yard and stood picking strands of smelly hay off her clothes.

'Phew! Anyone got a spare clothes

peg?' Penny said, holding her nose.

'Oh, shut up!' Tash fumed, looking
daggers at her. 'You think you're so clever,
don't you, Penny Cookson? Well, we'll see
who has the last laugh!'

'Uh-oh,' Lindsey whispered worriedly
to Comet. 'I don't like the sound of that.'

Chapter
SEVEN

Despite Lindsey's fears, nothing else happened between Tash and Penny. In fact they appeared to be ignoring each other. *Which is probably for the best*, she thought.

By the following afternoon the rain had stopped and the yard had dried out a bit. Lindsey watched as Allsorts trotted round in a circle while Gina held him on a lunge rein.

'Show Allsorts what you want him
to do, see? That's how you get a pony
to adjust his stride. Now you try,' the
instructor handed her the rein.

Lindsey took it and did as she'd been
shown. Allsorts obligingly lengthened
his stride and cantered round in a wider
circle.

'That's it. Well done,' Gina praised.

Lindsey smiled, proud of the way
Allsorts held himself as she put him
through his paces. She would miss the
little pony very much.

The rest of the day passed quickly. And
just before supper, everyone went back to
their cabins to change out of their riding
kit.

Lindsey was taking her muddy boots
off when, from inside their cabin, Penny

gave a yell. 'My favourite model pony!
Petal the Palomino. She's gone!'

'Maybe you put her away somewhere,'
Lindsey suggested.

'No, I didn't. Petal was right here on
my bedside chest with all the others this
morning!' Penny opened drawers and
peered under the bed.

'I'll help you look,' Lindsey offered.

She and Penny practically turned the cabin upside down, but there was no sign of the tiny palomino pony.

By now, Penny was close to tears. 'Someone's taken her. And I know who! Tash!'

Lindsey suspected that Penny might be right. She'd been afraid of something like this happening. 'Let's go and tell Gina Morgan,' she suggested.

Penny swallowed, crestfallen. 'What's the point? We haven't got any proof. Besides, I've never been a snitch and I'm not starting now.'

'You could ask Tash and see what she says. Maybe she'll give Petal back if she sees how upset you are,' Lindsey suggested.

'I wouldn't hold your breath,' Penny

said bleakly. 'She can't stand me. And I feel the same way about her.' She took a big breath and wiped her eyes. 'Well – I'm not going to let her see me cry. Would you come with me to the film room? It's *National Treasure* – one of my favourites. And it's all about a rescued racehorse, so it's bound to cheer me up in the meantime.'

Lindsey's heart sank. She'd promised to meet Comet, but how could she leave Penny now when she was upset and needed her – especially after riding off the other day? She racked her brains trying to think of a solution as she walked towards the main building with Penny.

The film was really good, but Lindsey couldn't concentrate. All she could think

of was Comet waiting for her in the
woods.

After a while, she leaned over to
whisper in Penny's ear. 'I've got a
headache coming on and I . . . um, feel a
bit sick. I think I'll go back to the cabin.'

'Poor you. I'll come and look after you,'
Penny said at once.

'Don't worry' Lindsey whispered
hastily. 'Thanks, but I'll be fine. I'll
probably just go to sleep. You stay and
watch the film. I'll see you later.'

'Well, OK then. If you're sure,' Penny said.

Lindsey nodded and slipped outside,
leaving Penny engrossed in the film.
She set off in the direction of the woods
and found Comet waiting patiently. He
whinnied softly and took a step towards
her.

'Hi, Comet.' She reached out to stroke his silky dark-brown neck. 'Sorry I'm late. I only just managed to get away.'

'You are here now. Thank you, Lins,' Comet neighed, tossing his head. 'Climb on to my back.'

Excitement stirred inside Lindsey as she mounted Comet and took a firm grip on his mane, nudging him on with her heels.

'Let's go!'

'Hold tight!' Comet snorted eagerly
and sprang forward into a gallop.

Lindsey crouched low on his back,
moving in time to his strides, and
her breath caught in her throat with
excitement as they raced along. Comet
was thrilling to ride, so smooth and fast.
His magic seemed to swirl around her, as
he flew along, his shining hooves barely
touching the grass.

Moonlight silvered the trees and the
woods were a map of shadows. It was
very quiet. With no one else around it
could have been a bit creepy, but Lindsey
felt perfectly safe with Comet.

They left the woods and flashed across
fields, soaring up and down hills and
valleys with dizzying speed, looking for

Destiny. But they saw no signs of any ponies.

'Let's try over there.' Lindsey pointed to Hamilton Hall, the stately stone house that she'd seen on the hill when her parents first drove her to pony camp.

After exploring the large gardens and grounds of Hamilton Hall, Comet headed for the lake. His hooves made no sound as they crossed a stone bridge. He paused and bent his head to the moonlit water that was as smooth as a deep-blue mirror. Ripples spread outwards as he drank.

Lindsey looked around her. The ghostly cry of an owl echoed in the still air. She felt as if there was no one else in the world except her and Comet. And she knew she would remember this special night for as long as she lived.

'We'd better go back soon,' Lindsey said
regretfully. She could happily have ridden
Comet for the entire night, but the film
show would soon be over. When Shawna,
Tash and Penny returned to the cabin
they were bound to notice if she wasn't in
bed.

Comet nodded. Pricking up his ears he
headed across the fields and back to the
woods. But as he approached the trees,
Lindsey felt him stiffen. He stopped and

leaned down to stare at the grass.

Lindsey looked down too. In front of them and stretching away into the distance was a faint line of softly glowing violet hoof-prints.

'Destiny! She came this way!' Comet whinnied excitedly.

Lindsey felt a pang. Did that mean that he was going to leave, right now? 'Do you want me to get down, so you can go after her?' she asked anxiously.

Comet shook his head. 'No, Lins. This trail is cold. But it proves Destiny was here.' He pricked his ears forward again with fresh hope. 'When she is very close I will be able to hear her hoof-beats. And then I may have to leave suddenly, without saying goodbye.'

'Oh.' Lindsey didn't think she could

bear it if that happened. She knew that she had to face up to the fact that Comet could not stay forever, but she would never be ready to lose her magical friend.

Comet snuffled Destiny's trail for a moment longer, lingering over the faint scent. Lindsey was touched by how much he missed his twin sister. He must love her very much. She leaned forward to pat his neck.

Raising his head, Comet shook himself. 'I will take you back,' he snorted.

Flicking his tail, he moved up into a full gallop and, once again, his long strides ate up the ground. In no time at all, the fields and woods were behind them and the cabin came into view.

Lindsey dismounted at the edge of the wood. She put her arms round Comet's neck and laid her cheek against his warm neck. Comet blew out warm breath and nuzzled her shoulder very gently.

She moved away reluctantly. 'Night, Comet. I'll see you tomorrow.'

'Goodnight, Lins.'

As she walked away, he melted into the trees.

As Lindsey reached the cabin, the door opened and Penny flew out. 'Lins! I came back to see if you were OK. And you weren't here. Where have you been?'

'I felt . . . um, a bit better, so I . . . um, went out for some fresh air.' Lindsey stumbled over the hasty explanation. It wasn't exactly a fib. She *had* gulped huge lungfuls of fresh air while out riding Comet.

'But you were gone ages. I was just about to go and tell Gina Morgan that I couldn't find you!'

'Sorry,' Lindsey murmured. 'I just lost track of time.'

Penny smiled, looking relieved. 'Oh, well, you're back now. Let's go inside. We have to get up early tomorrow. It's cross-country, remember?'

'Oh, yes!' Lindsey was looking forward to it. Allsorts loved jumping. It would be fun to see how well the plucky little pony did over a whole course of fences.

Inside the cabin, Penny gathered up her model ponies, and she and Lindsey had a game of making them gallop over humps in the duvet.

'I wish I knew where Petal the Palomino is,' Penny said, looking downcast. 'She was so pretty. My gran bought her for my last birthday. I hate to think she might have been thrown away and I'll never see her again.'

'Petal will turn up, you'll see,' Lindsey said, hoping it was true.

She still felt sure that Tash knew something about Penny's missing model, but she had denied all knowledge when Penny had asked her. Even if she had something to do with Petal's disappearance, Lindsey knew Tash would never admit it.

'Phew!' Lindsey breathed, as she dismounted in the yard the following afternoon. She was hot and sticky and couldn't wait to take off her body-protector and riding hat.

Penny rode up on Chance. 'That was brilliant. I love cross-country. Allsorts did really well.' She slid down and tethered the blue-roan pony.

'Yes, he did, didn't he?' Lindsey agreed proudly, sliding up the stirrups and undoing the girth straps. 'He even gave Jewel a run for his money. Did you see

Tash scowling at us?'

'It was hard to tell. She's always scowling,' Penny said.

They both laughed.

'I can't believe that tomorrow's our last day,' Lindsey said.

She was surprised by how glum she felt at the thought of leaving and she knew it wasn't just about losing Allsorts soon. She and Penny had become really good friends. And what was going to happen to Comet? Lindsey couldn't bear to leave him behind, sad and lonely and still looking for his lost twin sister.

'I know. The week's flown past, hasn't it?' Penny said. She waved a hand in front of Lindsey's face. 'Hello? Are you listening?'

'Oh, sorry,' Lindsey said, smiling, as she lifted off the heavy saddle. 'I was miles away.'

They carried their saddles and bridles into the tack room and then returned to hose down the sweaty ponies.

'Actually, Lins, there's something I've been meaning to ask you.' Penny grinned, swooshing water off Chance's rump with a cupped hand. 'You know that I'm going to be moving to Blakestone? Well, I have a favour to ask . . .'

Chapter
EIGHT

Lindsey didn't have a single moment to herself for the rest of the day. After lunch there were team games. Pony-relay, sack race and then a catch-the-train race. The sight of Penny struggling into a floppy old-fashioned hat and baggy red dress, before running up to Chance and leaping on to her back, was just too much! Lindsey laughed until her ribs ached.

Then in the evening there was a team treasure hunt, followed by karaoke, and once again it was impossible for Lindsey to get away. She decided that she would have to wait until everyone was asleep before going to meet Comet.

She lay in bed staring into the semi-darkness as Tash and Shawna chatted and giggled annoyingly. But soon, despite their noise, her eyes started to droop.

Lindsey woke hours later to twittering birdsong. 'Oh, no! It's almost light!' she murmured. Throwing back the duvet, she quickly checked the other girls were asleep, before tiptoeing outside.

'Comet!' she whispered, as she entered the wood. 'Are you there?'

He appeared immediately at the edge of the woods. Morning mist swirled around his legs, and the white star on his forehead stood out against his dark-brown coat. Snorting affectionately, he trotted to meet her.

Lindsey felt a deep thrill of wonder and excitement when she saw him. She knew she'd never take being Comet's friend for granted. He was her special secret, never to be told to anyone else.

The magic pony whickered softly and

leaned forward, so that she could put her arms round his neck. 'I haven't got long. The others will be waking up soon, but I just had to see you. I've got some news!' she told him.

As she stood back, Comet blinked. 'Has something happened?'

'Yes!' Lindsey exclaimed, bursting with excitement. 'It's Penny. She's asked me if I wanted to share her pony, Chance. I said I'd love to. She's moving close to me, so I'll be able to see her every day. We'll both look after Chance and take turns riding her. Isn't that amazing?'

Comet nuzzled her affectionately. 'Yes. It is wonderful news.'

But there was also something else Lindsey needed to tell Comet. She wasn't looking forward to it, but she couldn't put it off any longer. 'After the prize-giving for most-improved rider, everyone will be leaving pony camp to go back home. I would love it so much if you would come back and live with me. But . . . but I don't think you can, can you?' she asked sadly.

Comet's violet eyes glistened, but he lifted his head proudly. 'No. I must continue my search for Destiny. She is close – but do not worry about me, Lins.'

But she knew she *would* worry. She couldn't help it. Sadness at the thought of leaving without him washed over her.

Part of her felt as if she had let Comet down in some way, although she knew she had done her best to keep her promise to him. She sighed; if only she could be certain that the lonely pony would be reunited with his lost sister. It would be awful never to know.

After giving Comet a final hug, Lindsey was about to slip quietly back into the cabin, when she had a sudden thought. 'Penny's still really upset because her model pony hasn't turned up. Petal the Palomino was her favourite. I'd love to find it for her. Do you think you could help me?'

'It would be my pleasure.'

Almost at once, Lindsey felt a familiar prickling sensation flowing to her fingertips as violet sparkles twinkled in Comet's mane and tail and he blew out a big breath that turned into a glittering rainbow mist. As she stared at the mist, a picture formed of Tash's shoulder bag in the wardrobe. Tucked away in the toe of a sock, right in the bottom, was a tiny model pony.

'Petal! I knew it!' Lindsey burst out crossly. 'How mean is that girl? Thank you, Comet.'

'You are welcome,' Comet neighed, as every last spark faded and the rainbow mist blew away across the grass like glittering dust.

'I'll see you later!' Lindsey said. She had something she had to do.

Chapter
NINE

Lindsey crept back into the cabin and carefully opened the wardrobe. It creaked loudly and she paused, wincing as she looked over her shoulder. Luckily her cabin-mates were still asleep.

She quickly finished what she was doing, before closing the wardrobe door. Grabbing some clean clothes, she darted into the bathroom and had showered and

dressed by the time the other girls were
up and about.

'It's no good getting up early to groom
that scruffy black-and-white pony. You
won't win the prize for most-improved
rider!' Tash jeered, pulling on her riding
boots.

'That's right. You haven't got a chance!
Tash always wins that prize,' Shawna said.

'Whatever.' Lindsey shrugged as she bit
back a grin.

'Yeow! What's sticking into me?'
Suddenly Tash gave a loud yell, as she
pulled off her right boot. She tipped it up
and a small object fell out.

'Petal! Yay!' Penny cried, snatching up
her tiny palomino pony.

'What's that doing in there? It was in
my ba– I mean, someone must have put it

there,' Tash burbled guiltily.

Penny squared her shoulders and
looked Tash in the eye. 'I knew you'd
pinched her. Don't ever try that again
– or else!'

Tash backed away warily. 'But it wasn't
me! I didn't –'

'Don't bother,' Penny said coldly, walking away. 'Come on, Lins. Let's go and see Chance and Allsorts before breakfast.'

Later in the Hay Net there was fresh orange juice and American-style pancakes with maple syrup for a special treat. Afterwards, everyone trooped to the tack room for the prize-giving.

Lindsey breathed in the smells of leather and saddle soap, as she and Penny perched on blanket boxes with the other kids. Lindsey heard a soft neigh and looked round to see Comet's head poking in through the open window.

She smiled at her friend as Gina Morgan began speaking. 'The prize isn't just for the most-improved rider. It's also for the rider who's been the best team–player and the most helpful . . .'

Suddenly Lindsey heard a sound she'd been both hoping for and dreading at the same time.

The hollow sound of galloping hooves overhead.

She froze. Destiny! It had to be.

Comet had gone. She heard his eager whinny and knew he was following the magical hoof-beats that were getting louder and closer.

'I'll be right back!' she whispered to Penny, before jumping up and rushing outside.

As she rounded the building, there was a flash and twinkling rainbow mist floated down around Comet. He stood there in his true form, a handsome dark-brown

pony with a white star no longer, but a
magnificent cream pony with a noble
head and proudly arched neck. His
flowing mane and tail and gold-feathered
wings gleamed brightly in the sunshine.

'Comet!' Lindsey gasped. She had
almost forgotten how beautiful he was.
'Hurry! You have to catch her!' she cried,
forcing herself to swallow the lump that

rose in her throat.

Comet's deep violet eyes softened with affection. 'Farewell. You have been a good friend.'

'I'll never forget you,' she said, her voice breaking. It was hard to let him go, even though she knew this had to happen.

Comet spread his magnificent gold wings. 'I will not forget you either. Ride well and true, Lindsey,' he said in a deep musical neigh.

Lindsey rushed forward, threw her arms round his silky neck and pressed her face to his glowing warmth for one last time. And then she slowly backed away.

There was a final flash of bright violet light and a silent burst of rainbow crystals that showered down around her and tinkled like tiny bells as they hit the ground.

Comet soared upwards. He faded and was gone.

Lindsey stood there, fighting tears. She could hardly believe how fast it had happened. Something glittered on the ground. It was a single shimmering gold wing-feather. As she bent and picked it up, it tingled faintly against her palm and turned to a cream colour.

She put it in her pocket, knowing she would always treasure it as a reminder of her wonderful magical friend. After a moment, she took a deep breath and tried very hard not to feel so sad. This was what she had hoped would happen. Comet had found his sister. Now she wouldn't worry about leaving him here all alone.

She walked back to the tack room, just as Penny rushed out to meet her. 'There you are! Gina's looking for you. You won the prize!'

'Really?' Lindsey said in delight, starting to smile in amazement. 'I bet Tash's furious.'

'She is! Gina's giving her a severe lecture about being a bad loser!' Penny said triumphantly. 'Look, my mum and dad have just arrived. Let's go and tell them our news!'

Lindsey found herself beaming.
Everything had worked out perfectly.
'Thank you for everything, Comet.
I hope you and Destiny get home safely
to Rainbow Mist Island!'